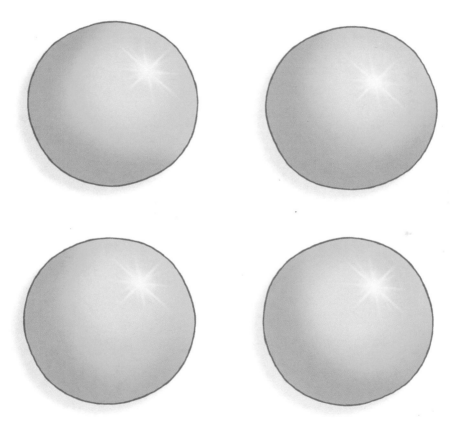

Dedicated to my
wonderful wife,
my two beautiful boys,
and to my gorgeous
girl Sofia who also
likes to do twirls.
..Roberto

Dedicated to my Mom,
who picked up after
my twirling ...
and to my Pop,
who fed my twirling
habit with ballet lessons.
..Silvia

published by SalixEyas
1st edition July 2013
copyright © Di Falco/Hoefnagels
ISBN 978-1-491-00121-9
printed and bound by CreateSpace

The Girl With the Funny Buttons
by Roberto Di Falco
illustrated by Silvia Hoefnagels

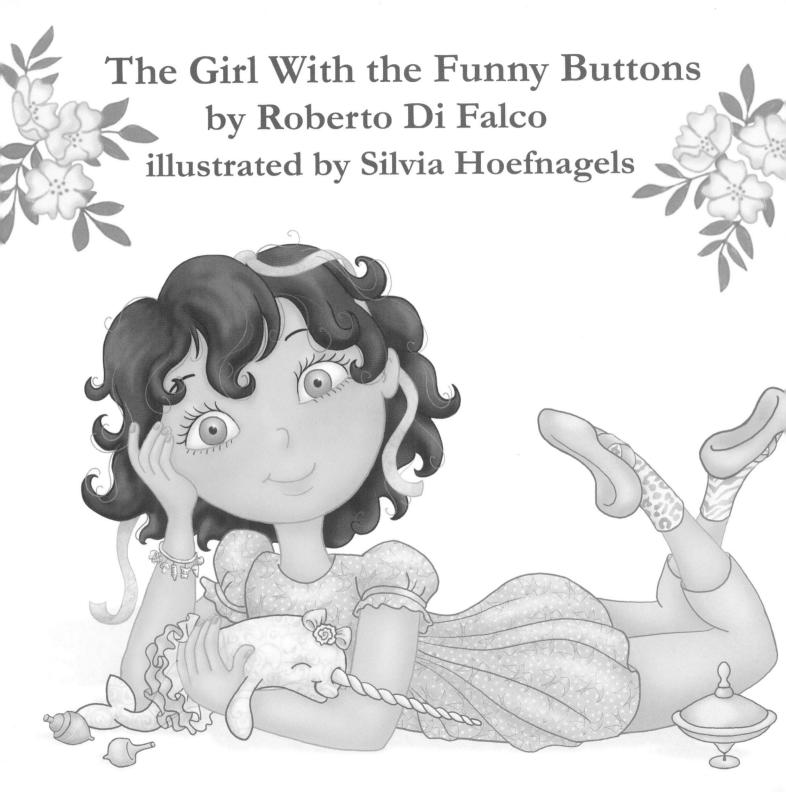

There was this young girl
Who liked to do twirls
When she put on her favourite top.
She would raise up her nose
And stand on her toes
And the twirling would just never stop.

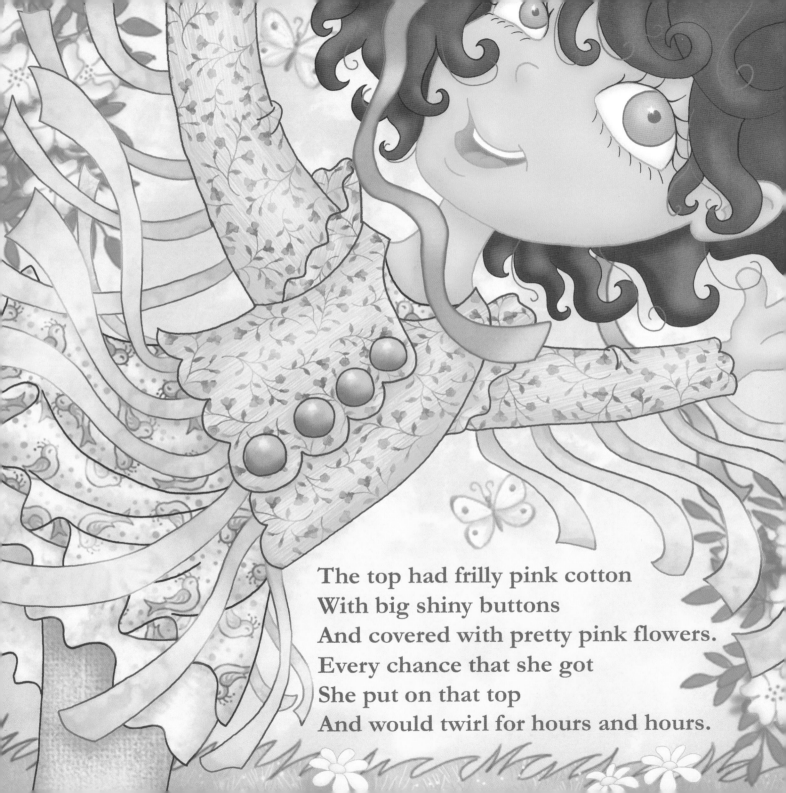

The top had frilly pink cotton
With big shiny buttons
And covered with pretty pink flowers.
Every chance that she got
She put on that top
And would twirl for hours and hours.

Each week that went by
Her mummy would cry
"We must give that top a good clean"
So the top would come off
To be put in the wash
And for that day it wouldn't be seen.

The girl would then wait
That bit she did hate;
Eager to twirl in her favourite top.
When the cleaning was done
She would put the top on...
But this time a twirl she did not.

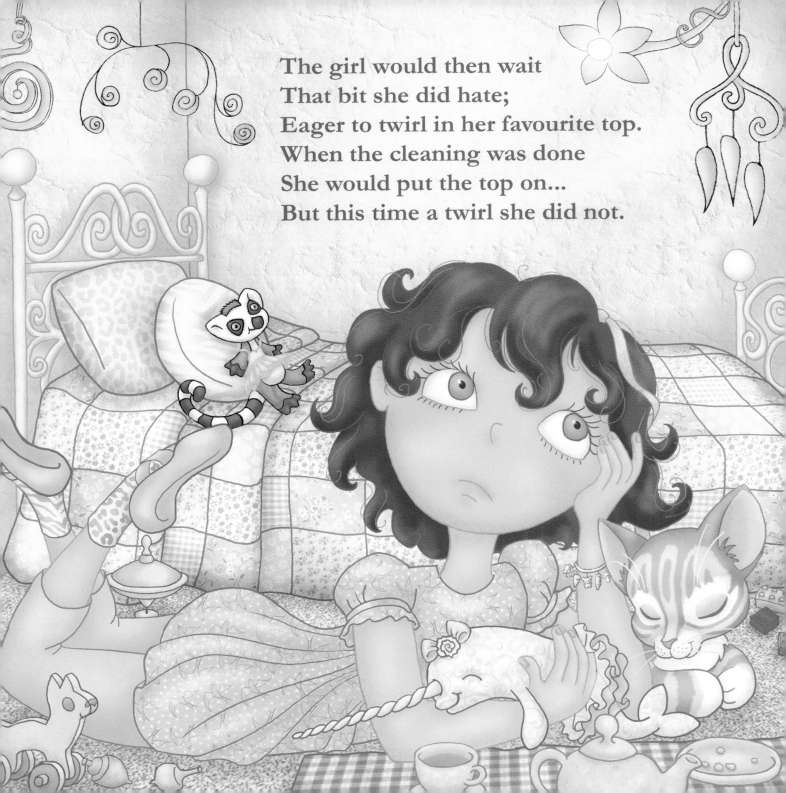

This time she frowned
For when she looked down
The problem was immediately seen
The shiny buttons had gone
And replaced with new ones
They were red, blue, yellow and green

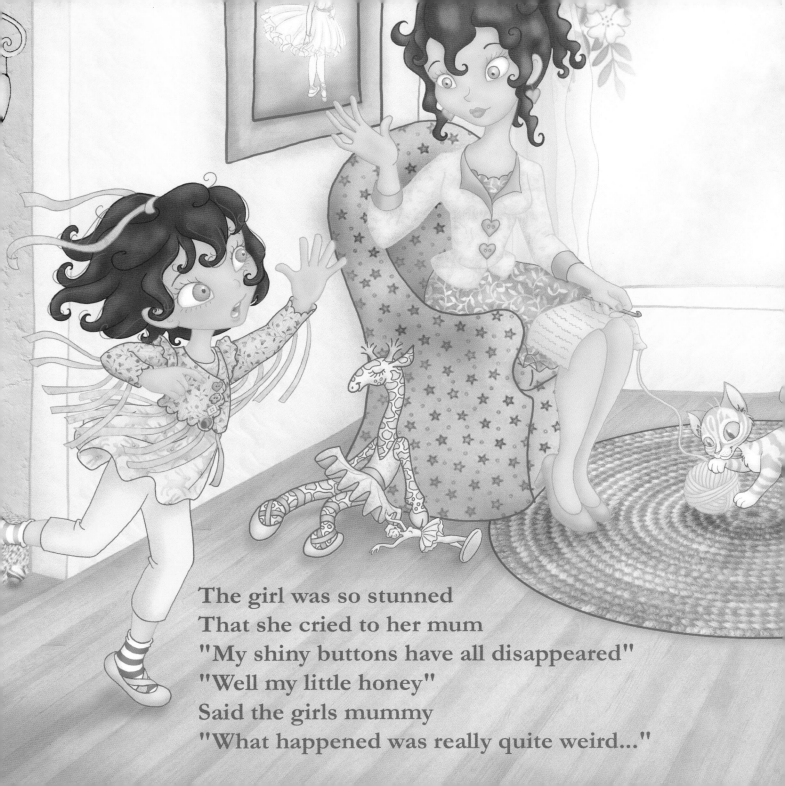

The girl was so stunned
That she cried to her mum
"My shiny buttons have all disappeared"
"Well my little honey"
Said the girls mummy
"What happened was really quite weird..."

"The first button fell off
And was caught by a moth
Which flew high and got stuck in a web.
When I then reached for it
My own button unstitched
So I used my red button instead."

"You are silly Mummy
That's not very funny"
Cried the girl that now wouldn't twirl.
"But now you've confessed
What about the rest?"
Cried the now very curious girl.

"Well, it really is funny
Because I lost my money
When I took the clothes to the laundrette,
So I used a button off your top
And put that in the machine slot
Then replaced it with a blue one instead"

"You are silly Mummy
That's a little bit funny"
Sniffed the girl that now wouldn't twirl.
"So that's red and blue
What about the last two?"
Sniffed the now very curious girl.

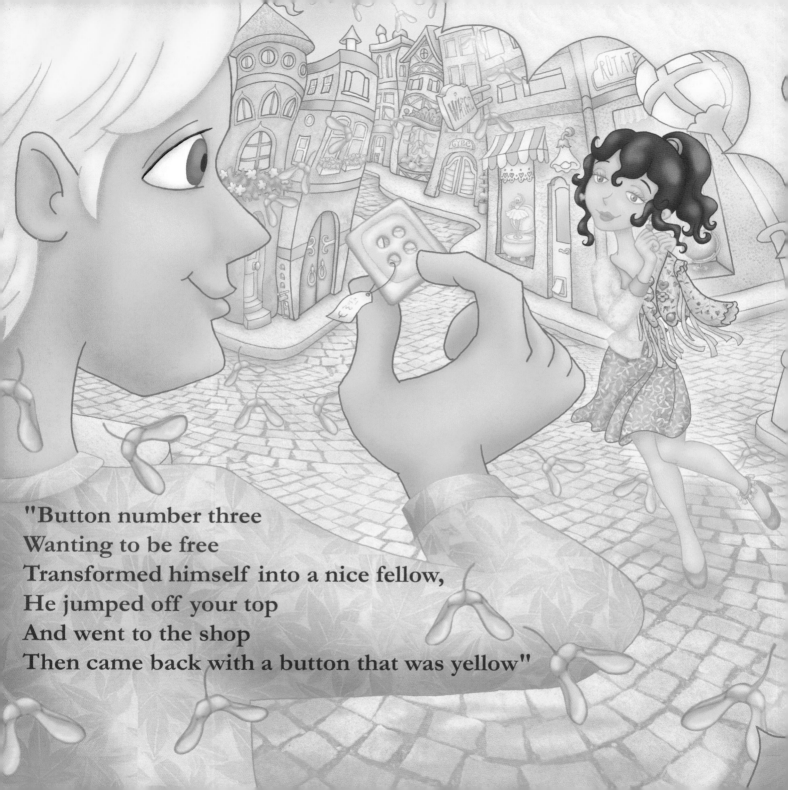

"Button number three
Wanting to be free
Transformed himself into a nice fellow,
He jumped off your top
And went to the shop
Then came back with a button that was yellow"

"You are silly Mummy
Now that is getting funny"
Said the girl that now wouldn't twirl.
"That's now three buttons gone
What about the last one?"
Said the now very curious girl.

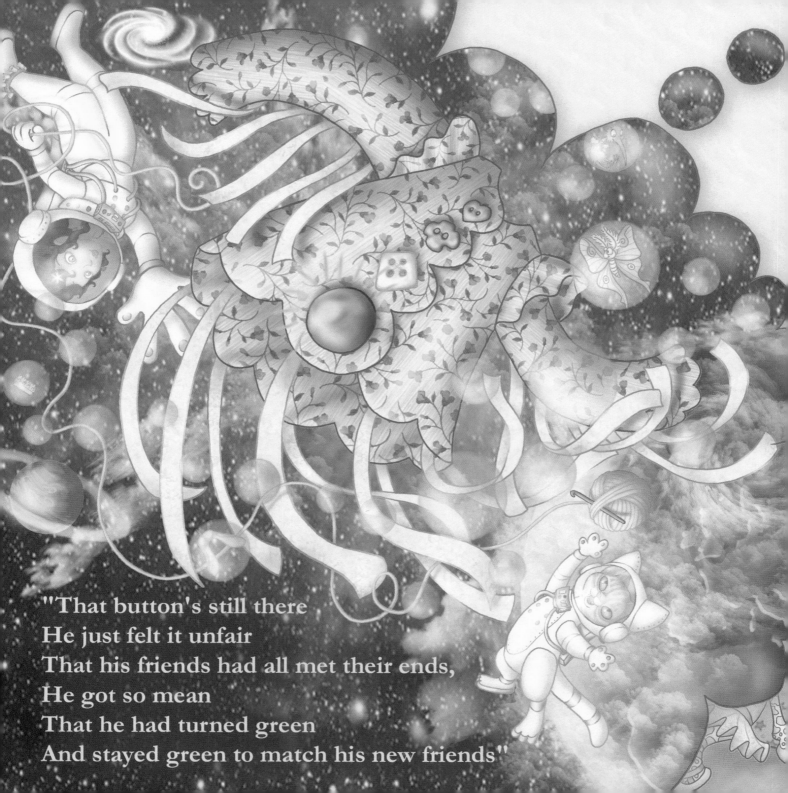

"That button's still there
He just felt it unfair
That his friends had all met their ends,
He got so mean
That he had turned green
And stayed green to match his new friends"

"You are silly Mummy
That is very funny"
Laughed the girl that now wouldn't twirl.
"You see" said the mum
"You're no longer glum
So why don't you give us a whirl?"

So she raised up her nose
And stood on her toes
And gave it another shot.

Then without strain
She was twirling again
Because it was still
her favourite top.

The End

coming soon:

by Roberto:
"The Boy in the Tree"
"The Silly Sneeze"

by Silvia:
"Eye No" (book 2 of Elfleda-Fae and Kiwi-Sprite)

a special thanks to Michael Becker,
gisticator assemblage realizer

ballet art in picture frames inspired by
Edgar Degas and Pierre-Auguste Renoir

SalixEyas
2013

published by
SalixEyas 2013

SalixEyas blog: salixeyas.blogspot.ie

Made in the USA
Charleston, SC
30 May 2014